The JOLLEY-ROGERS
and the
CAVE of
DOOM

For Nana and Grandpa:
for the baked Alaska, lemon drizzle and all
those sunny days at the seaside.

A TEMPLAR BOOK

First published in the UK in 2015 by Templar Publishing,

part of the Bonnier Publishing Group,

The Plaza, 535 King's Road,

London, SW10 0SZ

www.templarco.co.uk

www.bonnierpublishing.com

ISBN 978-1-84877-241-0

3 4 5 6 7 8 9 10

Printed in the UK

The JOLLEY-ROGERS
and the
CAVE of
DOOM

JONNY DUDDLE

templar

Thrice the cursed cat has mew'd!
Once or twice the old pig oink'd!
Seagulls cry: 'Tis time! 'Tis time!

Hubble, flubble, toil and trouble, Lanterns burn and cauldron bubble. Bring us pirates at the double!

Crab claws, shells and brains of snails, Seaweed, pebbles, fish entrails! Candy floss and ice-cream cones, Chopped off heads of fishing gnomes!
Biscuits, maggots, hair of dog, Half a pint of old man's grog, Fish and chips and mushy peas, Seagulls' beaks and knobbly knees!

Verrucas, boils, corns and bunions,
Hotdog buns with sauce and onions,
Sweets and treats and all things nice,
Weevils, warts and fat head lice!

Mix it, stir it, warm it through, Sprinkle brine and puffin poo!
Add some drops of monkey blood, Then the curse is firm and good!

Come hither scurvy sea dogs! Come see our cave of gold!
Come hither, beneath the Hag's Head! Let our treasure take its hold!

1.
Scurvy Sea Dogs

"We be needin' a day at the beach!" said Mr Jolley-Rogers. He wasn't entirely sure why he said it. He just did. He'd been planning to tar the deadeyes, but he suddenly had the strangest urge to build a sand ship.

"I was thinkin' the same thing," said Mrs Jolley-Rogers who, moments earlier, had told Nugget that it wasn't sunny enough for a day at the beach.

"BRILLIANT!" said Nugget, who

was plucking maggots from an old ship's biscuit and making them into a living, wriggling, necklace. It had been fun at first, but the maggots kept squirming free and falling down her pinafore dress. If they went to the beach, she could collect shells and seaweed and make a much less wriggly necklace.

Nugget's big brother, Jim Lad, appeared from below decks. "Where we headin', Dad?"

"This be lookin' like a good spot," said Mr Jolley-Rogers. He noticed his finger was already pointing to the map. "ℍMMM, Hag's Head. I'll plot a course. Who wants to take the helm?"

"ARRR!" shouted Nugget, as she hopped onto a barrel, grabbing the wheel with one hand whilst itching her bottom with the other. Squawk, the parrot, flapped around her feet, feasting on the maggots that were raining onto the deck.

Jim Lad scurried aloft with a telescope. His mum was already dropping the foresail. Dad flipped the lid of the ship's compass, tore open a bag of toffees and hollered, "North-east for Hag's Head!"

"LAND AHOY!" yelled Jim Lad from the crow's nest, a few hours later. It was a bit blustery aloft and had started to drizzle, and Jim's fingers were going numb as he hurriedly furled the topsail. "Perfect beach weather..." he thought, as he slid down a rope to join the rest of his family on deck.

"I'll be stayin' put," said Grandpa, creaking back and forth on his rocking chair with a frown and a large bottle of grog in his good hand. Grandpa rarely left the ship. He claimed never to have set foot on dry land, since his right hand was chopped off by the king many years ago as punishment for being a pirate. Jim wasn't sure if he believed him.

"You won't get me on dry land. I'll be stickin' to these old timbers. I might take a nap whilst yer all ashore. But be warned, me hearties. Watch out for lubbers!"

"WATCH OUT FOR LUBBERS!" echoed Squawk, perched on Grandpa's shoulder.

The Jolley-Rogers headed below decks to the hold, where

their amphibious jeep was chained to the floor, leaving Grandpa grumbling about untrustworthy landlubbers. Jim's dad set about unlocking the chains, while Jim, his mum and Nugget picked out their beach things from the shelves and cupboards.

"Why do we need so much stuff?" grumbled Jim's dad, ten minutes later. He had loaded twelve towels, a beach ball, a frisbee, surfboards, bodyboards, a windbreak, two coolboxes and a plastic bag (oozing suntan lotions) onto the back of the jeep. "There's barely room for my metal detector. Is Bones coming too?"

"WOOF," said Bones and hopped onto Jim's knee.

Jim strapped Bones in and whispered, "HOLD TIGHT!"

Dad turned the key and the jeep's engine rumbled. Mum pressed the remote control to open the ramp at the stern of the ship and, with a cloud of exhaust smoke, the jeep hurtled out of the Blackhole and into the air. They hit the water with a **SPLASH**.

"I'm soaked!" laughed Jim Lad.

The windscreen wipers flip-flapped, Nugget declared her maggots "lost at sea" and the jeep's propeller gurgled to life, churning seawater as they bobbed towards the shore.

2.
A Day at the Beach

"Well," said Jim's dad, flopped on a beach mat. "Isn't this nice?"

Nobody could hear him. Nugget was out of earshot, rockpooling with Bones, and Jim and his mum were surfing, just visible over the top of the windbreak. Jim's dad poured the last dribble of warm grog from his flask into a plastic mug, and gulped it down. He'd finished the wordsearch in the *Pirate Times,* and it was a bit cloudy for sunbathing. "What shall I do now?" he muttered. "HMMM... I think I'll get the metal detector out."

Jim's dad loved his metal detector. It made treasure hunting so much easier. He was rubbish at measuring steps and always got his left and right confused, so treasure maps were tricky to follow.

Not that he'd ever found any treasure. "I've got a good feeling about this beach," he said to himself. "I can almost smell the gold."

Before long, Jim's dad had his headphones on, and was swinging his metal detector left and right across the sand. He wasn't sure why, but a cave had grabbed his attention. He had an irresistible urge to walk towards it, and everything seemed to be going a bit hazy.

From outside his headphones, he heard the faint sound of Nugget asking if she could come too. He wasn't sure if he answered her, but he felt her fingers encircle his thumb, as they strolled into the darkness.

"BEEP!" went the metal detector. "BEEEP! BEEEEEP! BEEEEEEEEEEEEEEEEEEP!"

"What's all that barking about?" said Jim.

Jim and his mum were waist-deep in the surf, clutching their boards, but Bones had grabbed their attention. He was bouncing excitedly around on the shoreline. "WOOF! WOOF! WOOF!"

"ARRRR, I dunno, but Bones don't normally get so agitated," said Mum. "I can't see Dad or Nugget. Maybe we'd best go and see..."

They waded ashore, boards under their arms, and stopped where their stuff lay abandoned in the middle of the beach.

"COME 'ERE, BONES!" called Jim, but Bones kept on running, towards the rocks. He barked and dived into a cave, then poked his head out and barked again. "You dry yerself or ye'll catch yer death of cold," said Mum. "And I'll go see what's got him so worked up…"

Jim changed out of his wetsuit, while his mum followed Bones to the cave's entrance. He watched as they both entered the cave but, moments later, only Bones emerged. He was barking again, running back to Jim as fast as his peg leg could carry him.

"What is it, Bones?" said Jim. "Where's Mum? Are Dad and Nugget in there too?"

But Bones was off again, across the sand towards the cave. Jim chased after him, buckling his belt as he ran.

Jim peered into the cave. It was tall and deep, and curved into inky blackness, beads of water dribbling down the jagged rocks on either side. There was no sign of

Nugget and his parents, just three sets of footprints heading into the unknown. Something wasn't right.

"BONES," said Jim, with some urgency, pulling a scrap of paper and a stubby pencil from his pocket. "I'm writin' this note for Matilda. If I don't come out of this cave, if there's somethin' fishy goin' on, take this note to her. Y'hear?"

"WOOF!" said Bones.

"Dull-on-Sea is north of 'ere. Take that path up the cliff, and follow the lanes to town. I'm sure there'll be a biscuit in it for yer. Ye'll find Matilda's house, won't yer?"

Bones wagged his tail and nodded. Jim

pulled some thread from his sash and tied the note to Bones' collar, good and tight. Jim Lad's best friend, Matilda, was a landlubber. And she didn't live too far away, in the sleepy seaside town of Dull-on-Sea. If something happened to him, he was sure she would come to help.

"Right," said Jim. "You wait here! If I ain't back in five minutes, you go get Matilda. Good dog!"

Bones wagged his tail again and waited.
And waited.
And waited a little bit longer.

But Jim didn't
come back.

3.
DEAR TILLY

It was the summer holidays, but the weather was doing its best to make it feel like autumn. Matilda was painting at her kitchen table, with the patio door open onto the garden. She'd just finished a sea monster that she was quite pleased with and was wondering what to paint next.

WOOF!

Matilda looked up to see a dog in the garden. She didn't even have a dog, so that was strange. Stranger still, Matilda's cat, Fluff, trotted past her and into the garden. Fluff usually hated dogs.

Matilda jumped up to see Fluff pushing her face up against the dog's cheeks and curling her tail around his ears. This wasn't any old dog, it was a pirate dog! It was Bones! He was Fluff's sweetheart, and also the faithful companion of Matilda's best friend and pirate pen-pal, Jim Lad.

"Is Jim here?" asked Matilda, a little overcome with excitement because she hadn't seen Jim for ages.

"ARF...." said Bones and shook his head. Matilda noticed a roll of paper wobbling on his collar. She bent down and untied it.

"Oh no!" Matilda cried. "Bones, can you take me there?" Bones nodded his head and tapped his wooden leg on the patio.

Matilda's dad was building a model aeroplane in the study and her mum had caught the bus to town. Matilda ran inside and grabbed her coat, a water bottle, a map, her pocket money (just in case) and a couple of biscuits.

"Dad, I'm going out on my bike!" shouted Matilda as she ran past the study door. Her dad was busy trying to unstick a tiny transparent cockpit canopy from his thumb but there was glue everywhere, and he could only mumble, "Oh... okay. Don't go too far!"

Matilda flipped a biscuit to Bones and pulled her bike out of the shed, quickly donning her helmet and stuffing everything else in an old rucksack.

"Fancy a lift...?" she said, placing Bones in the basket on her handlebars. Then she hopped on her bike, pushed off through her gate and sped along the road, pedalling as hard and fast as she could. Fluff watched wistfully from the gatepost.

1.
THE CAVE

Matilda dropped her bike to the grass. Bones had already jumped from her basket and had disappeared over the edge of the cliff. There was a path, but it was overgrown and, if Bones hadn't taken it, Matilda could quite easily have ridden by.

Looking over the edge of the cliff, she could see Bones bounding over the rocks towards a cave, which cut deep beneath the headland. In the middle of the sand, Matilda noticed the Jolley-Rogers' beach things.

Their jeep was parked wheel-deep in the surf. It looked like the family had been there moments before, but now they were nowhere to be seen. She felt a shiver run down her spine.

Matilda rolled down her sleeves, so the gorse and brambles wouldn't scratch her. She fought her way through the heavy undergrowth at the top of the path, pushing prickly branches above her head, and trying to avoid the nettles that sprung out around her ankles. Halfway down, she had to cross a very rickety bridge, with broken handrails entwined in foliage.

Soon she was at Bones' side, peering into the darkness. Bones looked at her, then looked in the cave. Then looked at her again, wagging his tail.

The cave looked
very dark.

Bones gave one last bark,
and disappeared inside.

Matilda took a deep breath,
and walked slowly into the shadows.

As her eyes adjusted to the darkness, Matilda could make out a faint yellow glow from deep within the cave. She turned a corner and the rocks lit up with the flickering light of lanterns, bouncing in all directions off a huge hoard of gold. Great piles of gold coins, goblets, crowns and jewellery covered the sand. Wooden chests and caskets lay open, overflowing with treasure. Matilda gasped.

It was only then that she noticed the Jolley-Rogers, standing before the great pile of gold, with their backs to her. Bones bounded towards them.

"Hello..." said Matilda, from a distance. "Jim...?"

There was no answer. Not one of them turned to greet her. Bones was tugging at Jim's sash, but Jim was motionless.

His body shook a little as Bones tugged, but his feet were rooted to the spot. Matilda took a deep breath and crept forward...

She walked in front of the Jolley-Rogers and said "hello" again, but still nobody moved. The expressions on their faces remained exactly the same. They were all staring blankly at the booty, mouths hanging open. Jim's dad had a metal detector, which was making a faint, broken crackling noise.

Matilda waved her arms in the air, jumped up and down and shouted, "Heeeellooooo Jooolleeeey-Rogeeerrrrs!"

Nothing.

Bones whimpered with his head bowed.

Matilda poked Jim in the tummy. He didn't flinch.

"Jim, can you hear me?" she said. He didn't speak, he didn't nod, but something in his eyes told her that Jim could hear her voice.

"Are you okay?"

She tickled him under his chin. Nothing. She poked him in the tummy again. Nothing. Matilda put her nose right up against Jim's and said, "Boo!"

His eyes definitely flicked downwards for a split second. But nothing else moved.

"So you are there! Why won't you talk to me?" she shouted. Then she noticed Bones. He was pulling on Jim's sash again, his paws and peg leg kicking up sand as his body jerked back and forth. His little growls were muffled by the fabric.

"Bones... Do we need to get Jim out of the cave?"

"WOOF!" said Bones.

Matilda stood behind Jim, and put her arms under his, wrapping them tightly around his chest. She leant back and pulled. Jim felt like a lead weight, his body limp and his arms swinging loosely by his sides, while Matilda dragged him backwards across the sand. Bones helped as best he could, teeth clenched on Jim's sash.

Jim's head started to move a little, and mumbled words fell from his lips. Matilda's heart was beating hard against her ribs. Jim was heavy and, although it hadn't seemed far walking into the cave, pulling him the same distance was tough.

Stumbling backwards into the daylight, they all collapsed in a heap.

5.
THE SPELL IS BROKEN

Jim Lad sat bolt upright. Bones jumped up and licked his face, his tail wagging furiously. Jim turned around, pulled Matilda up off the sand and hugged her so hard she thought she'd burst.

"MATILDA!" said Jim. "I knew ye'd come!"

"What happened?" asked Matilda. "Why did none of you move?"

"I couldn't," said Jim. "My folks had gone in there, but none had returned.

So I followed 'em. Everythin' went hazy and I couldn't stop me'self! Just kept on walkin' against me wishes. Then, when I saw that treasure, I froze. Stuck still. Couldn't move a muscle. There's a curse, f'sure...

"Yer a good dog, Bones!" Jim ruffled Bones' head. "If we was all bewitched by that gold, how come you were alright? And Bones too?"

"I don't know," said Matilda. "Maybe it's because you're a pirate, and I'm not. And Bones is a dog. Or something..."

Jim looked back at the cave, and stood up. "We've gotta go back for my folks!"

"But you can't go back, Jim," said Matilda. "Wouldn't you fall under the spell again? I'd never be able to move them on my own. Me and Bones could barely drag you. I'm sure he won't mind me saying, your dad looks a lot heavier than you."

"Then I'll head to the Blackhole and get some ropes," said Jim, pointing towards the Jolley Rogers' ship, shrouded in sea spray out in the bay.

"With a block and tackle, we could yank 'em all out at once. You could go in and lash 'em up, then we could pull 'em out together from the beach!"

"I suppose that might work," said

Matilda. "Or we could go up to that house and ask if we could use their phone..."

Matilda pointed to an old, ramshackle house that she hadn't noticed before. It was perched precariously on the cliff, directly above the cave. But Jim had already gone, running across the beach. Matilda watched him pick up a surfboard and paddle, and then he was off over the waves, standing on his board, paddling towards the Blackhole.

Matilda shrugged and looked at Bones. "Maybe we should go and rescue Nugget..."

Feeling a little more brave, Matilda and Bones walked back into the cave.

The rest of Jim's family were just as they'd left them.

"Same again...?" Matilda said to Bones. But as she went to put her arms around Nugget, she heard footsteps.

Matilda squinted through the flickering light, beyond the treasure, and saw stone steps leading up into the darkness. She could just make out three pairs of feet hopping from one step to another. Matilda looked back towards the entrance of the cave, but there was no time to get out. She would surely be spotted.

Bones jumped behind a rock and Matilda followed him. Crouching in the darkness, they heard voices getting closer.

"We heard woofs!" said one.

"We did!" cackled another.

"An 'orrible dog, perhaps...?" said the third, who was glancing around the rocks with a lantern swinging from her raised hand. "Dogs is good for potions... They've got tongues and claws and fluffy paws..."

"Better than that!" they all shrieked together, when they spotted the Jolley-Rogers. "We got some scurvy pirates!"

6.
THE SEA HAGS

"Oh, we is lucky old sea hags!" said the first hag. "Years it has been, no pirates we've seen..."

"I like this little one," said the second. "She looks plump and tasty!"

"Can we make her into stew?" said the third, licking her lips.

Matilda's foot was in a puddle and her toes were going numb. She tried shifting her weight and had to put her hand out to balance, but it came to rest on something that didn't feel at all like rock. It was smooth and cold. She turned and saw a skull, amongst a pile of bones. "Eww!" she cried. The hags whipped around. Matilda heard their feet shuffling closer across the sand.

Do we have a visitor?
Another pirate, perhaps?
Come out, Mister Pirate! Come out to play! Oh, we are lucky girls today!
Do you not like our lovely gold? Did you manage to break the hold?
Cowering in the rocks won't help... A rat amongst the bones and kelp...

A withered hand wrenched Matilda from her hiding place. The next moment, she was engulfed in shadow as three figures surrounded her. Three long, wart-encrusted noses twitched, then sniffed at her. Six beady eyes glared at her. Behind the eyes, there were three great clouds of hair. Matilda was terrified.

"She doesn't look like she came from the sea.
Looks like a lubber between you, you and me!"
"Take her up to the house we could..."
"Keep her!"
"Keep her!"
"Keep her, we should!"

She tried to speak, but no words came out. She just wanted to go home. Matilda turned to look at the Jolley-Rogers. All their eyes were looking back at her. But they couldn't help her. And Jim wouldn't be able to come back into the cave.

Suddenly, with an almighty "WOOF!", Bones sprang from behind the rocks, flying towards the hags, fierce and determined...

But in mid-air he froze, floating in a fizzing ball of light. The second hag held a wand in her outstretched hand, green light streaming from its tip, and as she moved it, Bones moved too.

"Look at his tongue!
His tongue!
His tongue!

So very pink! So very long!"
"Perfect for potions! Perfect for spells!
Although without it, he'll NOT bark so well...."

The sea hags cackled and shrieked and made their way up the steps, with a wide-eyed Bones, suspended in a ball of light, and Matilda flung over the third hag's shoulder.

7.
HAG'S HEAD HOUSE

Up, up, the twisting staircase they went, until finally Matilda and the sea hags emerged from a tiny doorway cut into the side of the rock.

"Here we are, have a seat!" said the third hag, dumping Matilda on the hard, slate floor. "Take your weight from off my feet!"

Matilda looked around nervously. She was in an enormous room. Three walls supported cupboards and shelves, buckling under the weight of books, boxes, bottles and jars. A pale-looking monkey sat in a cage suspended from the ceiling. Other cages, jars and glass tanks held an assortment of glum-looking animals.

The opposite side of the room was almost entirely a window, which looked like it had been cobbled together from hundreds of different glass panes, with a view across the bay and out to sea.

One of the hags dragged over a small cage. The second hag dropped Bones into it and the light that surrounded him fizzled out. She slammed the lid shut. Bones jumped up and started growling, which made the three hags cackle some more.

"Growl little dog,
while you still have a tongue!
Enjoy how it feels, it won't be for long!"

The sea hags turned to Matilda, crowding around her, bent double, hands curled like claws.

"This is our house, sea hags are we,
Witches you'd say, who live by the sea."
"This is my sister!"
"My sister is she!"
"My sister is that one!"
"Sisters are we!"
"My name is Dabberlocks!"
"My name is Maerl!"
"I've been called Pipweed, since I was a girl!"

Suddenly, Dabberlocks stood straight with a finger raised in the air.

"If there are pirates, there must be a ship!" she said, hobbling over to a long brass telescope on a wooden tripod by the window. "A ship! A ship! There we are! Find me a bung! Find me a jar!"

Her sisters rummaged in a cupboard. Pipweed handed her a huge jar, Maerl a matching cork, and Dabberlocks trotted purposefully outside, through a double door in the wall of windows.

"She'll be back, she won't go far! Gone to collect a ship in a jar!" said Pipweed.

"We don't always talk in rhyme, y'know... Sometimes we just can't be bothered," said Maerl. "Cup of tea, sister dear?"

"Oh, yes. That would be lovely," said Pipweed.

They turned back to Matilda and hoisted her onto her feet.

"Show her the kitchen, show her the pot!"
"Show the selection of tea bags we've got!"

Matilda was hustled out of the room and into a kitchen at the back of the house. Maerl put the kettle on the hob and Pipweed opened a cupboard. They did indeed have a wide selection of tea bags.

8.
SHIPS IN BOTTLES

Half an hour later, the two sisters had just finished explaining to Matilda which teabags which witch liked to drink at which particular time of day.

"When I fancy something a little more potent than peppermint tea, you can't beat a hot frogspawn infusion," said Pipweed as she slurped the dregs from her cup.

"More cake, dear?"

"Oh, no thank you," said Matilda. "I'm quite full up." She'd eaten a substantial amount of Victoria sponge and two thick slices of banana loaf, washed down with blackberry tea, but she hadn't liked the look of the slug gateau. The hags had told her that it was a special treat for Dabberlocks' three hundred and forty-fifth birthday. Matilda was pretty sure they had lost count.

"Dabberlocks was much cheerier before she was three hundred!" said Pipweed, pulling a stretchy piece of slug from between her teeth. "Now she's all grumpy and bossy and dabbling in darkness all the time..."

Matilda had enjoyed her tea and cake, but the whole time she had been worrying about the Jolley-Rogers, bewitched in the cave beneath the house, and how she was going to rescue them. And what would Jim Lad think when he came back from the ship and she wasn't there?

But the hags were actually very nice once you got know them. They seemed to like Matilda too. Matilda finally plucked up the courage to say something.

"Erm... Excuse me, but why do you want the pirates?" she asked. "The ones in the cave...?"

"Ooooh, we'll show you our collections!" they chirped.

They took Matilda to Pipweed's bedroom. Every inch of wall space was decorated with pirate flags. Hundreds of Jolly Rogers filled the room. The bed had a patchwork skull blanket, there was an armchair upholstered in flags, and the curtains were a great long flag cut in two. "I DO LOVE A NICE JOLLY ROGER!" said Pipweed, clenching her palms together.

They shuffled along the corridor to Maerl's bedroom. The room was lined with shelves from floor to ceiling, and every shelf was brimful of pirate hats. Matilda thought she knew what a pirate hat looked like, but she'd never seen ones like this before.

Some had feathers, some were embroidered with skulls, while others were decorated with gold trim. Many were black, but there were reds and purples and deep crimsons, too. "I can't resist a nice hat," said Maerl, blushing.

"And pirates do have the BEST hats."

They headed to a third bedroom, and found Dabberlocks, out of breath, clutching the large bottle which now contained an incredibly detailed model of a pirate ship. Matilda thought it looked remarkably like the Jolley-Rogers' ship, the Blackhole.

"I found this bobbing in the sea!" said Dabberlocks. "I think I'll rearrange. I always like to keep a new ship on a low shelf, so I can look at it properly!"

Dabberlocks' room was lined with shelves, just like Maerl's, but instead of hats they overflowed with hundreds of model ships inside bottles and jars.

"I used to construct the ships myself," she said. "But I found it was much easier to get them *ready-made*."

This made her sisters chuckle.

"Ready-made?" thought Matilda. It seemed an odd thing to say. But then she looked at the ship and something terrible entered her mind. "Oh no! Dabberlocks found it 'bobbing in the sea'! What if the new model ship was actually *the* Blackhole, magically shrunk down?"

Matilda tried to get a closer look but she couldn't get past Pipweed and Maerl, who were pointing through the glass and chattering excitedly.

"Erm... What wonderful collections," said Matilda. "And you have all that treasure in the cave, too. Why don't you put some of that on display?"

The hags screwed up their faces.

"Oooh, we don't like treasure!
We don't like gold!
Too bright and shiny, too yellow, too old!"
"But it's good to lure pirates,
and bring them to us,

We get hats, flags and ships, with minimum fuss."
"But we don't get so many as years ago.
Where they have gone, we just do not know..."

The hags' faces dropped, and they all looked terribly sad.

It was then that Matilda realised that the sea hags didn't even *want* all that gold. They probably didn't want the pirates either. They were just after pirate hats, flags and ships to add to their collections, and they were using the gold as bait! The hags were so alone on their windy cliff top, they didn't know there weren't many pirates left in the world. At least not the type with nice hats and Jolly-Roger flags.

And square-rig sailing ships...

If Dabberlocks' new ship really was the Blackhole, the Jolley-Rogers would never be able to escape the sea hags. She had to do something!

"If I can get you all the flags, hats and ships that you could ever want... Would you let my friends go?" Matilda asked.

The three hags huddled together, mumbling and sometimes sneaking a peek at her. Matilda started to worry that she should have kept quiet. She wasn't even sure her idea would work. She looked out to sea through Dabberlocks' dusty window, and wondered if Jim was on the beach, waiting for her.

All of a sudden, the sea hags turned to Matilda with beaming smiles.

"Oooh, yes! That would be good!
If you get us flags and hats, we would!"
"If ships you can find, happy we'd be!
No need to lure pirates in from the sea!"

"Brilliant!" said Matilda. "We'll need a bag of gold from the cave, and then we'll all catch a bus to Dull-on-Sea!"

But Matilda hadn't noticed that behind their backs, the sea hags all had their fingers crossed.

9.
A Trip to Town

Matilda was sitting between the three hags on the back seat of a bus. It was a small bus that ran along the coastal lanes between the beaches, villages and towns. There were a few locals mixed with holiday makers on the bus, but none of them wanted to be close to the sea hags. There were a couple of empty rows in front of Matilda, which meant there was space for her bicycle, which she'd rescued from the cliff top. Beyond the empty seats, a young girl, fingers gripping the seat back, peeked over the top, until her mum whispered something in her ear and turned her round to face the front. The sea hags were keeping their beady eyes on the large sack of treasure they'd left on the luggage rack.

Matilda thought she would be relieved to get off the bus. But once they stepped onto Dull-on-Sea High Street, even more people stared at the sea hags. Matilda locked her bike to some railings and they set off down the street, burly men nervously ducking into doorways and parents putting protective arms around their children. At least the sea hags were quiet, apart from their sack of gold clunking as they dragged it along the pavement. Matilda rushed them along as best she could, although they occasionally stopped to sniff a passer by, peer into a postbox with their illuminated wands or salvage stuff from bins.

Their first stop was a new shop called Gold-Diggerz, which promised to pay 'loads of cash' for any unwanted gold. It was a small shop, filled with a very fat man, bedecked in chunky jewellery and tapping away on a computer. He was sat at a leather-topped wooden desk, behind a nameplate which read: 'Harvey Carrot'. With the ring-a-ding of the door, he looked up.

"Well, hello," he boomed. "What can

I do for you... um... lovely... erm... ladies?"

Without a word, the sea hags emptied their sack of gold on the desk. If there had been enough space behind him, he would probably have fallen off his chair.

"Well, yes. Fancy that," he said, slapping his large, sweaty hands together. "That's quite a lot of gold isn't it?"

HARVEY
CARROT

"There's a lot more where that came from, Mr Carrot," said Matilda. Behind her, the hags stared at him, and sniffed the air.

"Really? Well, yes, how splendid, but please, call me Harvey..." he said, grinning. "And how much would you like for this little lot, young lady?"

"Five thousand pounds," said Matilda, as calmly as she could. She wasn't sure why she said it, but it was more money than she'd ever seen before, and it sounded like a LOT.

To Matilda's surprise, Harvey very quickly fumbled with his keys and unlocked a safe in the wall behind him.

He grabbed five big bundles of bank notes, and slapped them on the desk.

"A deal!" he said. "Five thousand pounds!"

Matilda felt very nervous with five thousand pounds stuffed in her rucksack. "Next stop... the bank!"

Matilda and the sea hags crossed the road to the Bank of Dull-on-Sea. She could hear them muttering between themselves about how their precious gold had been swapped for pieces of paper. They followed her into the bank, mumbling and cursing, and joined the queue. The bank was busy and Matilda thought they'd be waiting a very long time.

The hags peered around her, then huddled together, holding hands. They began a slow, whispered, rhythmic chant. One by one, the people in front of them in the queue stepped out of line, dazed and bewildered, and wandered out of the bank. In no time at all, Matilda and the sea hags were making their way to a cashier's window. Matilda could barely see over the counter.

"My friends would like to open a bank account," she said. "Can they make a deposit, please?"

Matilda shoved the five thousand pounds into the cashier's tray. The sea hags were so close behind her, their breath was steaming up the window.

The young man behind the glass

hurriedly counted the notes, before stashing them in his drawer and handing Matilda a receipt.

"Erm... If you'd all like to, erm, take a seat... um... A personal advisor will be with you... um... shortly.... To... um... open your account."

"We like you..." said the sea hags all at the same time, inches from the glass. They each gave the cashier a wink, before shuffling to their seats.

Half an hour later, the sea hags left the bank with a brand new bank account and a welcome pack. They each had a brightly coloured baseball cap too, emblazoned with 'Bank of Dull-on-Sea'.

10.
THE MAGICAL
INTERWEB!

Matilda and the sea hags went to Dull-on-Sea Library next. The library offered free internet, which was an important part of Matilda's plan. But first she had to teach the sea hags how to use a computer.

"It's not a real mouse," Matilda sighed. "It just looks a little bit like a mouse, because it's round and it has a cable which resembles a tail."

"OH," said the hags, all at once.

"It's a real mouse now!" said Pipweed, with a flash of her wand. Matilda watched what was now a very real mouse scurry off the edge of the desk.

It wasn't going well. A few zaps of the wand later and the mouse was back on the desk, made of plastic and attached to the computer. Weirdly, it did still have ears. Matilda decided to jump to the next step. Now the sea hags had opened a bank account, they could buy things online.

Matilda clicked open a web browser and, for added effect, span around on her chair, arms wide, which made the three hags jump.

"Ta da!" cried Matilda, pointing to the screen.

Maerl pulled out her wand in defence.

"Put that away!" said Matilda. "And stand back... Now I will show you my magic! This magic is so potent, I can make all that you desire appear at your door!"

"OOOOOOH!" said the sea hags.

"You can find the ship of your dreams! A beautiful hat!

The rarest of flags! And folk will come from afar and bring these things to Hag's Head House!" bellowed Matilda. "I call this the MAGICAL INTERWEB! Behold its power!"

"Shhh!" said the librarian.

Matilda searched for 'ship-in-a-bottle', and a beautiful ship popped up on the screen. It wasn't in a bottle, but it was a very impressive model, and she was sure the hags would have something to put it in. The sea hags moved closer, and Dabberlocks pointed her wand. "A ship! A ship!" she cried.

"And only three hundred and ninety-nine pounds!" said Matilda, hastily keying in the sea hags' bank details, and making sure she selected next-day delivery.

Matilda repeated her magic for the other two sisters, and had soon ordered a ship, a Jolly Roger and a truly magnificent hat. She printed receipts for the sea hags with pictures of each purchase, and they clung to their print-outs, jabbering excitedly.

An elderly man next to them, who had overheard Matilda's 'magic', said, "Can you get me a mermaid?"

"Shhh!" said the librarian.

Outside the library, the sea hags seemed unhappy.

Matilda's plan was working perfectly, but they were not convinced.

"You gave our gold to the fat man,
his paper to the bank..."
"We've seen the magical interweb!
But still we've drawn a blank."
"You promised me a ship!"
"You promised me a hat!"
"You promised me a flag!"
"We sea hags smell a rat!"

"I know," sighed Matilda. "You don't have any of your stuff yet, but it will come tomorrow, I promise. That's the beauty of the magical interweb. We all need to go home and get some sleep, and tomorrow you will get your hat, your flag and your ship-in-a-bottle. Trust me!"

"Trust you?" "Trust you?" "Trust you, you say?"
"When you take our gold and give it away?"
"How do we know that you will return,
back to the Hag's Head? That's our concern..."

"Of course I'll return to Hag's Head," said Matilda. "Those pirates, frozen in your cave, are my friends. We have a deal, remember? I'll help you get everything you want, and you'll set my friends free. "

"Hmmm," they said together. "We did agree."

"A deal we had, we shall wait and see..."
"We should let the girl go home methinks..."
"Do you think?"
"Yes, I think..."
"Hmm, think, think, think..."
"Me thinks too... Do you?"

"Right!" said Matilda. She'd spotted an ice-cream van and hastily changed the subject. "Let's go and get some ice creams!"

The sea hags completely forgot their grumbles as they trotted over to the ice-cream van. Matilda spent the last of her pocket money on ice creams for everyone, then walked the sea hags to the bus stop. They clambered on the bus, slurping noisily, and Matilda waved them goodbye.

"Don't forget to get off at Hag's Head!" shouted Matilda. "Press the button when you want to stop!"

Matilda let out a huge sigh of relief. She sat on a bench and finished her cone, and wondered what the following day would bring. She looked out to sea for a while, running over all the things that might happen and what she would do. It was almost time for dinner – her mum and dad would be looking at the clock wondering where she was – so Matilda unlocked her bike and rode home.

11.
BOXES

Next morning, Matilda caught the bus back to Hag's Head. She was nervous as she knocked on the sea hags' door. She wondered if post had ever been delivered to Hag's Head House. She hadn't been able to put a postcode on the orders, because the sea hags didn't know if they had one. What if their stuff didn't turn up?

The door opened. All three hags stood in the doorway, looking a bit disappointed that it was only Matilda and not a delivery.

"Come in, deary," said Pipweed.

"Cup of tea?" said Maerl.

"I've just squeezed a toad!" added Dabberlocks.

"Um... can I just have blackberry tea again, please?" said Matilda.

They sat in the kitchen and drank tea. Thankfully the hags had made some fresh blueberry muffins, which Matilda enjoyed, while the three sisters polished off the leftover slug gateau. Matilda took this opportunity to explain how they could continue to sell gold, pay it into the bank and buy whatever they wanted on the magical interweb. They just needed to take the bus to Dull-on-Sea whenever they felt like adding to their collections. The hags nodded and looked at her blankly. Every now and again they would shuffle to a corner of the kitchen and chatter amongst themselves.

The wait seemed like an eternity. Matilda wondered how the Jolley-Rogers were doing, frozen in the cave. And where was Jim Lad?

Three blackberry teas later, there was a knock on the door, and the sea hags jumped from their chairs.

They all rushed into the hall, and Pipweed opened the door.

"BEHOLD!" she cried. "THE DELIVERER!"

A man holding three large boxes looked confused. "Only just," he mumbled. "Took me ages to find you. You weren't on my sat-nav, darlin'. Sign here, please."

Pipweed signed for the parcels and they all bowed before the bemused driver.

"Thank you, kind sir, for your generous gifts! Please return to your magical kingdom until we call you again!"

Moments later, the sea hags were joyfully opening their boxes.

Matilda had never felt so relieved. "So..." she said quietly. "Can you un-freeze my pirate friends, please?"

Suddenly, the mood turned dark. The sea hags' smiles had disappeared and they were glaring at Matilda under three furrowed brows.

"We're afraid to say,
we've changed our minds.
You really have been very kind."
"But your magic is too new for us!
We need some help to catch the bus!"

"We need a girl to sell our gold,
to help us, and do as she's told!"

With that, Pipweed and Maerl grabbed Matilda by the arms and shoved her in the pantry, while Dabberlocks took down a key from a hook. The door slammed and Matilda heard the key turn in the lock, followed by shrieks and cackles as the sea hags walked away from the door.

12.
LITTLE JIM

It was a bit chilly in the pantry. Matilda wasn't sure how long she'd been there, but she wasn't going to rescue the Jolley-Rogers if she was stuck in a food store. She wondered what the hags had planned for her. Maybe they'd freeze her too. Or use her tongue for potions. Or make Nugget and Matilda stew! Then the key clunked and the door opened to reveal all three hags, with a mop and bucket, a broom, and a very long feather duster.

The hags howled with laughter and handed Matilda a scroll. Matilda loosened the ribbon that bound it, and the list fell to the floor, revealing hundreds of chores.

Even with so much to do, Matilda was happy to get out of the pantry. Helping around the house might give her the opportunity to escape – and save the Jolley-Rogers. She mopped the kitchen floor, scrubbed the worktop and washed the cups and saucers. The sea hags had a large vegetable garden, and pigs and chickens too.

Matilda picked peas and dug up potatoes, carrots and onions. She collected the eggs and fed the pigs, all under the watchful eye of Pipweed, who was knitting in a deckchair in a wide-brimmed hat, the cursed cat on her lap.

Matilda spent the next hour in the kitchen, scrubbing potatoes, peeling carrots and chopping onions. She passed everything to Maerl, who was concocting a soup in a vast stock pot.

Next, she fed the animals in the observatory, the glass-walled room she'd been dumped in the day before. Amongst the mournful menagerie, Bones was still there, lying in the cage with his head on his paws. When he saw Matilda he jumped up and started wagging his tail. "Don't worry, Bones," whispered Matilda, as she pushed a bowl through the bars. "I'll hatch a plan. I'll get us out of here."

Then she noticed Dabberlocks' elbows, protruding from a tattered armchair by the window, where she was reading a thick, leather-bound book. The hag's head poked around the side of the chair.

"Have you dusted the hats?
The ships in my room?
Have you brushed the floors?
I gave you a broom!

Then you'll be back under lock and key,
While we all have a snooze
for an hour or three!"

Matilda headed for the bedrooms, collecting the broom, a dustpan and the feather duster on her way through the kitchen, where Maerl was stirring the soup, singing to herself. She paused and, as Matilda left the room, she called out,

"It'll be ready soon, won't be long!
I'll ring the bell at the end of my song!"

Matilda had been dying to have a proper look at Dabberlocks' new ship-in-a-bottle, the one that looked remarkably like the Jolley-Rogers' Blackhole, so she went straight to Dabberlocks' bedroom.

The new ship was on the bottom shelf, nearest the door. Matilda knelt down and peered inside. She dusted the glass to get a better view and there, on deck, was

a tiny figure in a rocking chair. It looked just like Jim's Grandpa! The figure's head was bowed and he appeared to be asleep. A parrot was perched on his shoulder, also with its eyes closed. With her palms on the glass, Matilda's eyes scanned the Blackhole. And then she saw him. A tiny figure was climbing up the rigging. He jumped into the crow's nest and waved. It was Jim!

Matilda grabbed the cork bung and, with a firm twist, pulled it free. Jim swung on a rope, somersaulted onto the foredeck, ran up the bowsprit and leapt onto Matilda's palm, which was waiting for him at the neck of the bottle.

"Jim!" said Matilda, thrilled to see her friend, even if he was smaller than normal. "Shhh! I don't want to wake Grandpa!"

said Jim. "He were up and 'bout for a while yesterday, but I hid his contact lens, so he was thinkin' we were moored in the bay. I told him the fog had rolled in. He'll be in a right bad mood if he wakes to find out he's been shrunk by a lubber! There's a witch, Matilda! A sea hag! She sleeps in yonder bed. She snores louder than Grandpa!"

"There are three of them!" said Matilda. "They're sisters. They're quite nice some of the time. I took them to Dull-on-Sea yesterday and gave them an internet lesson and bought them ice creams. But now they've decided to keep me here. Bones is locked up in a cage. And your mum, dad and Nugget are still in the cave, I think. We need to escape!"

CLANG!
CLANG!
CLANG!

"That must be lunchtime," said Matilda. "I'll have to go..."

"Take me with you, Tilly!" said Jim.

"Okay..." said Matilda, and carefully dropped Jim into the pocket of her apron.

13.
ESCAPE!

Matilda was worn out. It had been a busy morning. She wolfed down her soup. There was freshly

baked bread too, and Matilda secretly dropped a few crumbs into the pocket of her apron, for Jim to eat. The sea hags took a little longer to finish their soup, dipping their bread and chattering to each other. They sat back in their chairs with their hands across their tummies, looking sleepy and heavy lidded.

"We'll be having a nap, snoozing in bed,
We get a bit sleepy, once we've been fed...
Yawn..."

Dabberlocks took Matilda back to the pantry, lifted the key from its hook and locked the door. As soon as Matilda heard them leave the kitchen, she plucked Jim from her pocket and placed him on the floor.

"Dabberlocks told me that they sleep for 'an hour or three' in the afternoon," she said. "That might give us time to escape, if we can unlock this door."

Jim looked at the door. "You know what, Tilly, I reckon I could get me'self under the bottom of that door. Where's the key?"

"It's hanging by a rope," said Matilda. "On the wall, to the right. I could reach it, but you're a bit... erm... small."

"But I'm a pirate, Tilly, and I love

climbin'!" said Jim confidently, and crawled out of sight, beneath the door.

Out of the pantry, he spotted the key on a row of hooks fixed to the wall above the worktop. It was a long way up for a very little Jim. The first problem was scaling the kitchen cupboards. Jim needed a rope and a grappling hook. He surveyed the room. Under the table he could see a rusted teaspoon on the floor. He pulled at some loose thread on the table cloth, until it looked long enough to reach the worktop. He took his penknife from his belt and cut the thread, tying it to the teaspoon. It felt like the heaviest teaspoon ever and, unlike his normal grappling hook, it was smooth and rounded. But maybe he could get it to latch onto one of the drawer handles.

Jim lined himself up beneath the drawers, most of the coiled thread hanging from his left hand, while he spun the teaspoon in his right. He hurled the teaspoon upwards as hard and fast as he could. It clattered against the handle, balanced precariously on one edge. Jim tried to jiggle it into position, but it came loose and tumbled to the floor with a crash. He tried again, and exactly the same thing

happened. He wished he'd brought a shrunken grappling hook from the ship.

He was just about to try a third time when he heard a loud clunk from the back door. He glanced over. It was the cursed cat, poking its enormous head through a cat flap, and it was looking straight at him. Jim ran and didn't look back. He heard another couple of clunks, and the sound of claws scurrying on the tiled floor.

Jim ran into the next room, the observatory, and desperately looked for somewhere to hide. Then he saw Bones, sitting inside a cage.

"BONES!" cried Jim.

Bones' eyes lit up and he jumped against the door of his cage.

Jim dashed across the floor and began climbing the bars of the cage as fast as he could. He heard the door creak behind him, as the cat padded into the room. Its eyes narrowed as it caught sight of Jim, hanging from Bones' cage. Watching carefully, its tail swishing from side to side, it crouched, ready to pounce...

Jim unbolted the cage.

He had never seen a cat move so fast.

He didn't think he'd seen Bones move that fast either. The cursed cat shot through the cat flap and was very fortunate that Bones was too big to follow him.

Climbing onto the worktop was a lot easier with Bones. Jim just stood on his head, Bones jumped up against the cupboards and Jim strolled casually off his nose. He climbed onto the bread bin, unhooked the key and jumped back onto Bones' nose. Jim dropped to the floor and pushed the key under the door, and Matilda let herself out of the pantry.

"Thank you, Jim!" Matilda squealed. "I wondered what was going on with all that commotion. Now we need to release your folks from the spell," she went on. Jim was standing on her palm, looking very pleased with himself. "You could get bewitched again too."

"I ain't worried 'bout that," said Jim. "Ye can just pop me in yer pocket, if that 'appens. I won't be as 'eavy as last time!"

"We also need to get you to the proper size. And then there's the Blackhole...."

"Which is in that old hag's bedroom," said Jim, looking a little less pleased.

"I think we're going to need the sea hags' spell book to undo the curse. The book is on the armchair in the observatory. One of them was reading it earlier, and I noticed she left her wand lying next to it.

We can grab them on the way out, but first we need the Blackhole." Matilda looked very serious. "You and Bones stay here, I'll creep in and grab the bottle. Get ready to run!"

Matilda was surprised that the sea hags hadn't woken up with all the noise in the kitchen, but when she got to Dabberlocks' room and heard how loudly she was snoring, it made more sense. Matilda crept in.

Luckily, the Blackhole was the nearest ship, on the lowest shelf. She carefully lifted it from its plinth and was about to step out of the room, when she noticed the sash window was raised slightly. And just outside, looking her way, was the cursed cat. It leapt through the billowing curtains and landed with a thump in the room. Matilda closed the door and ran.

"Quick!" she said to Jim. "The cat's in there! It'll wake the sea hags!"

They all tumbled into the observatory. Bones fetched Dabberlocks' wand and Matilda grabbed the spell book. She unbolted the door in the rock, and looked down the steep steps tumbling into the darkness towards the cave. Bones ran ahead, with Jim Lad on his back. Matilda shoved the door closed and wedged a broom between the handle and the rock. She hoped that would slow the sea hags down.

"GET OFF ME! GET OFF ME!" grumbled Dabberlocks. "CURSED CREATURE, LEAVE ME BE!"

The cat was pounding her blanket with its paws, mewing and purring and pushing against her. Dabberlocks rolled over and opened one eye.

"I need more time, cursed cat!
Get outside and chase a rat!"

She was just about to close her eye again when she noticed her new ship was missing.

"SISTERS!" she screamed, sitting up in bed. "IT'S GONE! THE SCURVY SHIP HAS GONE!"

11.
SPELLS AND POTIONS!

Matilda rushed down the steps. Her eyes adjusted to the dark as she went, until she reached the glowing lanterns in the cave below. The Jolley-Rogers were exactly how she'd left them the day before, staring blankly at the gold. Matilda carefully placed the glass bottle containing the Blackhole on the sand. She sat on a rock and opened the spell book. There was no contents page or index, so Matilda started leafing through, looking for anything to do with bewitching treasure.

Bones came over and dropped the wand at Matilda's feet, wagging his tail. Jim was still on Bones' back, clinging to his collar, with his eyes firmly closed and his fingers pinching his nose.

"Just in case I fall under the curse again," said Jim. "Ye found anythin', Tilly?"

"Not... yet..." said Matilda, flicking the pages with more urgency. "Aaah! Yes! Here's one for treasure... "

She picked up the wand from the floor

and, supporting the spell book on her other arm, pointed it at the treasure.

"Hocus pocus, gold doubloons, emeralds
and silver spoons,
Rubies, sapphires, diamond rings,
A treasure trove of shiny things!
Add some drops of parrot's blood,
Curse this treasure, Curse it good!"

Nothing happened, but then Matilda didn't have any parrot blood and Squawk was probably a bit little, at the moment, to ask him for any. It didn't sound right anyway. She needed to un-curse the treasure, not double-curse it.

"Maybe I need to find spells that don't list ingredients," she mumbled. "Hmm, this one sounds better...

Scurvy pirates, brave and bold,
Still beneath the treasure's hold.
Be still no more! Give flight to thee!
Do my bidding and be free!"

Jim's mum, dad and Nugget all started rising into the air. They still stared blankly at the treasure, but they floated up and up until their heads bumped against the cave roof. They just hung there, arms and legs dangling. "Hmm, that wasn't supposed to happen," said Matilda.

"No, it wasn't!" Jim Lad cried, clinging onto Bones' collar, with his legs floating above him, still squeezing his eyes tight shut.

"Ooops!" said Matilda. "I'll try the next one!"

Matilda looked at the next spell in the book, and noticed some scribbles at the bottom of the page. The handwriting was terrible, but she could just about read it: *"If pirates are to be unbound, the spell must then be rewound, one word*

and then another read, but in
reverse it should be said." Matilda
raised Dabberlocks' wand again, and
read the spell backwards.

"Will their against here them keep,
Still them hold, them tempt, them call,
Hypnotise will hoard treasure this,
Eyes yer damn, rubies and diamonds!"

The Jolley-Rogers plummeted to the ground.

"It worked!" yelled Matilda, delighted she'd broken the spell, even if it sounded silly and didn't rhyme.

"My head hurts!" said Nugget.

There was an almighty **CRACK** as the broom snapped at the top of the steps, and a **THUD** as the door slammed against the wall, followed by the cackling and cursing of the sea hags. Flashes of coloured light reflected off the walls, accompanied by the sound of clogs clattering downwards, towards the cave.

Pipweed and Maerl were either side of Dabberlocks, with their wands held aloft.

They stepped slowly towards Matilda and the Jolley-Rogers. Dabberlocks stared into Matilda's eyes, arm outstretched with beckoning fingers. "Come, little girl... give me my wand..."

BOOOOOM!

Several tiny cannonballs whizzed past Matilda's head and

crashed into the rocks and skeletons, throwing shards of bone and granite across the cave. Grandpa had woken up and was firing out of the neck of the bottle. He was still missing his contact lens, so his aim wasn't so good.

"GIANTS! GIANTS, EVERYWHERE!" he yelled. "ALL HANDS ON DECK!"

Grandpa fired another volley, and one cannonball knocked the skull off Pipweed's staff, while others smashed against the wall of the cave. The sea hags mumbled and cursed and ducked behind the boulders.

Matilda and the Jolley-Rogers took their chance to escape, darting towards the light at the cave entrance.

15.
THE SEA CHASE

They all rushed onto the beach. Jim was riding Bones, and his dad was running along with the Blackhole under his arm. Grandpa was still staggering about on the deck of the rolling ship, firing out the tiny cannonballs.

Each of them grabbed something from the pile of beach things on their way to the jeep, leaving only the windbreak flapping in the wind. They clambered aboard, fastening buckles as swiftly as they could. Jim's dad flicked the key and floored the accelerator, the jeep's wheels throwing up sand and pebbles as they surged into the water.

Jim Lad looked back towards the rocks and saw the three hags scurrying along a wooden jetty towards a small motor boat. Flashes and crackles followed them, like a miniature lightning storm. They had their boat untied in seconds. Thick clouds of smoke poured from the exhaust

as its engine gurgled into life. They turned it towards the jeep, and began to chase.

"You'd better be quick with them spells!" Jim said to Matilda. "They'll be on us quick enough..."

Matilda was frantically turning pages, pointing the wand at the Blackhole and muttering spells, but nothing was happening. All the time the sea hags were gaining on them. The jeep could travel on land and sea, but in the water it wasn't as quick as a proper boat.

The sea hags were getting closer. Dabberlocks was at the wheel, and her sisters were hanging over the sides, firing shards of lightning towards the Jolley-

Rogers, which exploded around them, showering sparks. They were travelling further and further from the shore, and the waves were getting bigger and bigger. Bow waves crashed over the front of the jeep and poured into the cabin, soaking everyone's feet.

"YER ALL GETTIN' A SOAKIN'!" laughed Jim, from his high point on the surfboard, on the back end of the jeep.

"Yeah, very funny..." grumbled Nugget. "Look out!"

Jim Lad ducked as a stream of light fizzed past his head. The jeep hit another wave and Jim lost his balance, falling into the sea water swilling about the footwell.

"Jim!" cried Matilda, and reached down to try and help him – but before she could pluck him from the water...

POP! Jim burst back to his normal size.

"It's the water!" cried Jim, pulling himself up. "The sea water reverses the spell! As soon as I hit the water, I felt the change!"

Matilda stuck the wand in her belt and reached for the Blackhole with both hands. She scooped up water in the bottle, where it poured around the shrunken ship, and quickly threw the whole thing overboard.

POP! The Blackhole shattered the glass bottle and burst back to its enormous, normal size, its sails immediately catching the wind.

"QUICK! THROW A LINE, JIM!"

yelled Dad.

Jim hurled a rope towards Grandpa, who was hanging over the rail of the Blackhole and still minus a contact lens, but he managed to grab the rope in his flapping arms. He quickly secured it to the windlass on deck, and the jeep was yanked across the water, safely out of reach of the sea hags.

"FULL SPEED AHEAD!"

hollered Grandpa, taking the helm of the Blackhole and tugging the Jolley-Rogers out to sea, leaving the sea hags bobbing and cursing in their wake.

16.
HOME

The clouds had parted and it was turning into a lovely evening, as the Blackhole arrived in Dull-on-Sea. Nugget steered the ship into port, the sails were furled, ropes were tied, and Jim and Matilda skipped down the gangplank.

"Thanks for yer help, Tilly!" said Jim Lad, sitting beside Matilda at the bus stop. "Them sea hags had us good and proper and we'd still be bewitched by that cursed gold, if ye'd not come to the rescue."

Matilda held Jim's hand. "No problem..." she said.

They sat in silence for a few moments, watching the sea, until the bus pulled up.

"Write me notes," said Matilda, turning to Jim as she climbed on board. Then she walked to the back of the bus and waved to Jim, for as long as she could see him, out of the dusty window.

Ten minutes later, Matilda walked in through the patio

door of her house. Her mum and dad were just sitting down to dinner.

"Where have you been?" said her dad. "You've been out all day, we were starting to worry. What have you been up to?"

"Stuff and things," said Matilda, tucking in. "Hanging out with Jim Lad mostly..."

After dinner, Matilda went up to her room and sat at her desk. Something poked her in the tummy, and it was only then she found Dabberlocks' wand still tucked in her belt. She pulled an exercise book from her drawer and grabbed a thick black felt-tip. She wrote 'A Guide to the Magical Interweb' on the cover, then opened the book and started writing.

Next morning, Matilda asked her dad for a large envelope, sealed the exercise book and wand inside, and wrote:

Pipweed, Maerl and Dabberlocks
Hag's Head House
Hag's Head
Dull-on-Sea
(Sorry I don't know the postcode.)

She doodled a skull and crossbones on the other side (she thought Pipweed might like it), and headed down the road to the postbox.

Don't miss Jim Lad and Matilda's
first swashbuckling adventure!

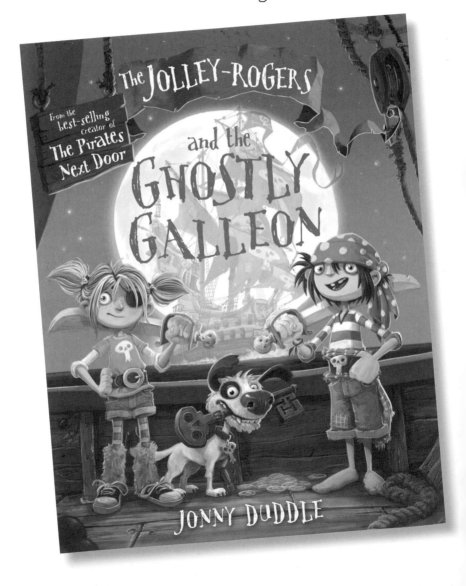